⚡The New Adventures of⚡
MARY-KATE & ASHLEY™

The Case Of The
Flying PHANTOM

This Book Belongs to

Kali Parr

Look for more great books in

series:

The Case Of The
Flying PHANTOM

by Melinda Metz

📖 HarperEntertainment
An Imprint of HarperCollins*Publishers*

A PARACHUTE PRESS BOOK

PARACHUTE PRESS

Parachute Publishing, L.L.C.
156 Fifth Avenue
New York, NY 10010

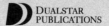 **DUALSTAR PUBLICATIONS**

Dualstar Publications
c/o Thorne and Company
A Professional Law Corporation
1801 Century Park East
Los Angeles, CA 90067

♨HarperEntertainment

An Imprint of HarperCollins*Publishers*
10 East 53rd Street, New York, NY 10022–5299

Aviator jackets courtesy of Avirex. Airplane cover photo courtesy of Michael Speciale.

ISBN 0-06-106591-9

HarperCollins®, ♨®, and HarperEntertainment™ are trademarks of
HarperCollins Publishers Inc.

First printing: July 2000

Printed in the United States of America

Outta site!
marykateandashley.com
Register Now

10 9 8 7 6 5 4 3 2 1

ALL SHOOK UP

"This place is too cool," Ashley said. We walked down a long hallway. Photos of funny old airplanes covered the walls.

Ashley and I had been dying to check out the Museum of Early Air Travel. We just couldn't end our trip to Washington, D.C. without seeing it.

A boy about our age with dark hair stood at a nearby T-shirt stand. He smiled at us. "I know exactly why you girls came

to the museum today," he said.

"You do?" we asked together.

"Yes," he said. "You came here because you need matching *Flying Phantom* T-shirts," he told us. "You're twins, right?"

I rolled my eyes at Ashley. She rolled her eyes back at me. We both have strawberry blond hair and blue eyes. We have the exact same nose and mouth, too. Even our ears look alike! So it's pretty clear to the whole world that we're twins.

The boy didn't wait for an answer. "I'm Jamie Duncan," he went on. "The Duncan brothers were my grandfather and great uncle. I'm the last living member of the Duncan family. At least I am now. My dad died when I was five."

"Who are the Duncan brothers?" I asked.

Jamie's dark brown eyes opened wide with shock. "Who are the Duncan brothers?" he cried. He seemed amazed that I didn't know.

I looked to Ashley. Had she ever heard of them? She shrugged and seemed just as clueless.

"The Duncan brothers built the *Flying Phantom*," Jamie explained. "It's the most famous World War I fighter plane ever built. It never lost a battle."

Jamie grabbed the top T-shirt off the pile. It had a photo of an old-fashioned plane printed on it. "*This* is the *Phantom*. It's a biplane. That's a plane that has two wings on each side."

A small, blond woman walked up. She put her arm around Jamie's shoulders. "Giving another lesson about the history of flying, Jamie?" she asked.

"He was telling us about the *Phantom*," Ashley told the woman.

"Hi. I'm Mrs. Duncan. Jamie's mom," she said. "I run the gift shop."

"But *I'm* in charge of the T-shirt stand, right?" Jamie asked.

"You're in charge for your whole summer vacation," Mrs. Duncan agreed. She leaned closer to Ashley and me. "Jamie has wanted a job since he was five. My boss finally agreed to let him work for me here."

"What's wrong with wanting to make money?" Jamie asked. "Money is what makes you rich—and I plan to be very rich some day."

Jamie's T-shirt had a picture of a hundred-dollar bill on the front. *He must like money a lot,* I thought.

Mrs. Duncan asked Jamie for five dollars worth of quarters. He gave it to her. Then she headed back into the gift shop.

"We have to go, too," Ashley said. She turned to me. "Let's see the *Phantom* first!"

"No!" Jamie cried. "You can't! Whatever you do—*don't* go in to see it!"

"Huh?" I said, confused.

"Just buy one of the T-shirts, okay? That's almost as good as going to see

the real thing," Jamie told us.

"What do you mean?" Ashley asked. She put her hands on her hips. "Why can't we see the plane?"

Jamie came out from behind the T-shirt stand. He stood close to Ashley and me. "It's haunted by the ghosts of the Duncan brothers," he told us. "You could get hurt if you go near it."

"We don't believe in ghosts," Ashley said firmly.

"Right," I added. But I wasn't as sure as Ashley. I've always thought ghosts *might* be real.

"You'll believe in ghosts if you go near the *Phantom*," Jamie warned. "If it were up to me, I'd get rid of that plane. Fast!"

"I want a T-shirt!" a little boy cried from behind me. He pushed his way between Ashley and me.

"Do you have children's sizes?" the boy's mother asked Jamie.

He gave her a big smile. "Sure do." He pulled a shirt out from the bottom of the pile.

"We're going to go inside, Jamie," Ashley told him. "Maybe we'll see you later."

Jamie shrugged. "Remember what I said," he said. The smile had disappeared from his face.

A little shiver went through me.

"A haunted plane, huh?" Ashley said as we started away from the T-shirt stand. She grabbed my arm. "Mary-Kate, I think Olsen and Olsen have found their next mystery."

That made me feel better. Thinking about ghosts gives me the creeps. But there's nothing more fun than solving a mystery.

I spotted a huge *Flying Phantom* banner hanging from the ceiling. The banner had a big arrow pointing to the left. "That's the way to our next case!" I told Ashley.

We walked down the hall as fast as we

could. Exhibit rooms opened up to either side, but we didn't even take a peek. We both wanted to see the *Phantom*.

"There it is!" Ashley cried. She pulled me into the last room and pointed toward the ceiling. The *Phantom* was hanging from thick metal cables.

I stared up at it. There were two wings on each side, stacked on top of each other. Fierce eyes were painted on the metal sides, toward the front. And it had a long, pointed nose with a propeller on the tip. It was as if the plane had a face with a black propeller mustache.

"Come join the group," a museum guide called to us. "I was just getting ready to tell these folks about the *Phantom*." He pointed to the tourists clustered around him.

Ashley and I hurried over. This was the perfect place to start learning about the *Phantom*.

"As I was saying, I'm Skip Henderson,"

the museum guide continued. "If there's anything you want to know about the *Phantom*, I'm the guy to ask."

"It looks like a regular old plane to me," I whispered to Ashley. "What's so scary about it?"

"I wish you folks could have seen the *Phantom* in the air," Skip went on. "The way this baby flew was amazing. The Duncan brothers designed it to be easy to control. It was better than any other plane of its time."

Ashley and I looked at one another and shrugged. So far, there was nothing creepy about the plane.

"The Duncans made their plane a two-seater," Skip told us. "That was something new back then. That way the pilot wouldn't have to worry about flying *and* working the machine guns."

I tried to imagine it was the middle of World War I. The *Phantom* was flying overhead doing loop-de-loops around enemy planes....

Suddenly, Ashley grabbed my arm. Then she squeezed it—hard. "Mary-Kate, look!" she said, pointing up at the plane.

The *Phantom* was shaking!

One of the tourists behind me gave a yelp of surprise.

"Everybody stay calm!" Skip called out. But he didn't sound calm. If you ask me, he sounded scared.

The *Phantom* shook harder. Then it started to rock. As we watched, the plane began to swing back and forth on its metal cables—all by itself!

The *Phantom* started to moan. You could hear the terrible sounds all over the room. And they were getting louder.

Planes don't moan, I told myself bravely. *Planes don't moan.*

But ghosts do!

2

NOT FOR SALE

The plane kept moaning.

"Let's get out of here!" a man yelled.

"We're right behind you," someone else shouted.

But Ashley and I didn't budge. I forced myself to keep staring up at the *Phantom*. I wanted to remember everything that was happening.

Suddenly the moaning stopped. Just like that.

The *Phantom* stopped rocking. But it

kept swinging on its cables. Each swing got a little shorter.

"Are you two all right?" Skip asked Ashley and me.

"Uh-huh," Ashley said. She already had her detective notebook out. Ashley is awesome that way. Nothing can stop her from taking her case notes.

Skip turned to an older man with white hair that stuck out in every direction. He was one of the tourists in the group. "What about you, Mr. Frost?"

"Aren't you going to tell someone in charge about this?" Mr. Frost demanded. He sounded really angry.

Skip nodded. He pulled out a walkie-talkie. "Terri, there's been another...um, event, in the *Phantom* exhibit."

"Be right there," a woman's voice answered.

Just then, Jamie burst into the room. "Didn't I tell you to stay out of here?" Jamie

cried. "I just heard what happened. You should have listened to me."

Before we could say anything, a tall woman walked into the room. "What happened this time, Skip?" she asked, tossing a long braid behind her shoulder.

"Well, first—" Skip began.

"Time out." The woman held up both hands. "This time, I think I'd like to hear a fresh opinion." She turned to Ashley and me. "I'm Terri Napoli, the museum director. That basically means I'm in charge around here." She smiled. "Would you please tell me what you saw?"

Ashley turned back a page in her detective notebook. "Well, I was looking at the portrait of the Duncan brothers painted on the side of the plane. And then—"

"And then it started rocking. And moaning!" I cut in.

Mr. Frost cleared his throat. "Don't you think it's time for you to consider my offer, Terri?" he asked. "These events are getting worse and worse. Soon no one will come to see the *Phantom*. And many people will be too scared to come to the museum at all."

"Yeah," Jamie jumped in. "I don't even like being in here with the *Phantom*. And *I'm a Duncan!*"

"I love the *Flying Phantom*," Skip said. "But there will be a lot of plane fans in town next weekend for the big air show. I'd hate for them to be too afraid to come to our museum."

"Mr. Frost, my answer is the same as before. The same as it always will be," Terri told him. "No. I will never sell you the *Phantom*."

"Why not?" Mr. Frost demanded to know. "I'm a very rich man."

I couldn't help looking at Jamie. He was listening closely. When Mr. Frost talked about how rich he was, his eyebrows rose.

He ran his fingers over the hundred-dollar bill printed on his T-shirt.

"Think of all the money I'll pay the museum for the *Phantom*," Mr. Frost went on. "You can buy six other planes."

"The *Phantom* is an important part of flying history," Terri said. "It belongs here—not in your private collection where no one will ever see it. Besides, if we sold the plane, the money wouldn't go to the museum anyway."

I glanced at Ashley. She was scribbling away again.

"What do you mean?" Mr. Frost demanded. A dark-red patch had appeared over each of his cheeks.

"If the museum ever sells the *Phantom*, the money will go to the remaining family of the Duncan brothers," Terri explained.

"Hey, that's me!" Jamie said. "*I'm* the last living Duncan!"

"I guess so," Terri told him. "Your mother

is a Duncan by marriage, so the money would go to you. She'd have to hold it in the bank for you until you were old enough, though."

"I can wait!" Jamie shouted. "Sooner or later I'd be rich!"

About a second later, Mr. Frost had his arm around Jamie's shoulders. "I think the two of us should have lunch. We'll invite your mother, of course. But you're the one I want to talk to."

He shot an annoyed glance at Terri. "You really should have told me this before. I wouldn't have wasted my time making you all those offers."

Terri shook her head. "No, Mr. Frost. You're wasting your time. Jamie doesn't have the right to sell you the *Phantom*. It belongs to the museum as long as we continue to exhibit it. That was the arrangement made when it was given to us many years ago."

I noticed a man and a woman with a little baby peer into the room. They shook their heads. Then they turned and left.

Mr. Frost noticed, too. "Whether the museum gets the money or not, it would be very smart of you to sell me the *Phantom*. A haunted plane is bad for business."

Jamie nodded.

"My sister and I are detectives," Ashley spoke up.

"I thought I'd seen you two before!" Terri exclaimed. "I saw your picture in a magazine. Olsen and Olsen, right?"

"Right," I said. "I'm Mary-Kate. And she's Ashley."

"And we'd both like to help you figure out exactly what is going on with the *Phantom*," Ashley added.

"We already know what's going on. It's haunted by the ghosts of the Duncan brothers," Skip said.

Ashley shook her head. "No way. There

has to be another reason these things are happening," she disagreed. "And I know Mary-Kate and I can find it."

"That would be wonderful!" Terri said.

"Are you two nuts?" Jamie burst out. "You want to mess with a ghost?"

"You girls should stay out of this," Mr. Frost added. "It could be very dangerous."

Ashley and I looked at each other. We'd never dropped a case because there was danger involved.

And we weren't going to start now.

3

CAUGHT RED-HANDED

"Let's go down to my office. There's something I want to show you," Terri told Ashley and me.

"Don't take the case!" Jamie cried as we walked toward the exit. "Mr. Frost is right. You could get hurt—or worse. Then I'd feel like it was my fault. After all, my grandfather and great-uncle built the plane. And they're the ones haunting it now!"

"We'll be fine," Ashley called over her shoulder.

"Oh, no!" Terri cried suddenly. "Not again! I'll be right back." She raced down the hall.

Ashley and I took one look at each other—then raced after her. Terri stopped in front of a red-haired woman wearing a long skirt. She had tons of crystal necklaces around her neck.

"Those things look heavy! I wonder if it's hard for her to stand up straight," Ashley whispered to me.

"Angelina, what have I told you about hanging out here?" Terri said to her. "You can't come to the museum and bother people. This is not the place to find customers for your business."

The woman pouted. "Terri, many people in this museum are having their first contact with the spirit world. Your ghosts are the first they've ever seen in action. They need my help to talk to them."

"The spirit world?" Ashley asked.

"Yes. Ghosts. Phantoms. The Other Side," the woman explained.

"What exactly do you do?" I wanted to know.

"I am Angelina Ritter," the woman answered. "I tell fortunes, read palms, and contact the spirit world for those on this side."

"Well, do it somewhere else, Angelina! I won't let you use this museum as your office," Terri told her.

"But I don't do my work here," Angelina argued. "I only find those in need of—"

Terri held up her hands. "No. That's all I have to say. *No!*"

"All right, all right," Angelina grumbled. "But before I go—let me contact the Duncan brothers. You need to find out what they want. It's the only way to put their spirits at rest. I can help you."

"I have all the help I need," Terri told the woman. "You can stay in the museum as

long as you'd like, Angelina. But if I see you bothering one more person with your business card—"

"Okay, okay," Angelina grumbled. She turned on her heel and stomped away.

"Sorry about that," Terri told us with a sigh.

She led Ashley and me into a small office. "The first thing I want to do is show you the videotape of one of the other so-called *hauntings*." She started hunting around on her desk.

"Could you tell us a little more about Mr. Frost?" I asked.

"Well, he's very rich," Terri said. "And he collects firsts. That's why he wants the *Phantom*. It's the first—and only—plane designed by the Duncan brothers."

"So he just collects planes?" Ashley asked.

Terri yanked open the top drawer of her desk and began searching through it. "No.

He's interested in any kind of first. He has the first pair of shoes that Johnny Sparkle the rock star ever wore on stage. The first television ever made. The first tooth the wrestler Buddy Juice lost in the ring."

She slammed the drawer and pulled open the next one. "Walter Frost won't be happy until he has the first one of everything. He doesn't understand that that's completely impossible. Ah-ha!"

Terri held up a videotape. "*This* is what I wanted to show you. Our security cameras tape everything that goes on in the different rooms. They run day and night."

Terri went over and put the tape in the VCR in the corner of the room. "The first two hauntings were pretty much like what you saw today," she explained. "But this one..."

She stopped speaking as a picture of the *Flying Phantom* filled the TV screen. It was hanging on its cables, completely still.

Then the moaning began.

Ashley gasped.

I shuddered.

The moans were horrible to hear. They sounded as if they were coming from someone in terrible pain.

I expected the plane to start rocking, just like before. But what happened next was even scarier.

Almost like magic, handprints appeared on the side of the *Phantom*.

Blood-red handprints!

4

MESSAGE FROM BEYOND

"**I** wonder where Jamie is," I said as Ashley and I headed back into the museum the next day.

"Waiting for you girls," Jamie said from behind us.

I turned and smiled at him. Today he wore a T-shirt with a piggy bank on it.

"I'm taking some time off from my T-shirt stand," Jamie told us. "I have to make sure you two don't get into any trouble."

"Do you try to protect everyone who

comes to visit the *Phantom*?" Ashley asked as we stepped inside.

"Most people are smart. They listen to me," Jamie went on. "And if they don't, they run away once they see the *Phantom* in action. But not you detectives."

We hurried down to the *Phantom* exhibit room. A thick velvet rope was strung in front of the door.

"Yes! We can't go in! Saved! Thank you!" Jamie exclaimed. He started to turn away.

"Not exactly," I told him. "We asked Terri to close the exhibit for the day. We need to look for clues."

Ashley and I stepped over the rope. Jamie followed us. But he didn't look happy.

"Good morning," Skip called from the far end of the room. "I hope you don't mind me butting in. I worry about you kids being in here by yourselves. It might not be safe. Not with what's been going on."

"We don't mind. Thanks," I said.

A teenage girl came to the entrance of the exhibit. She held a bunch of floating balloons in one hand. "Delivery for Skip Henderson," she called out.

"That's me," Skip answered.

"Is it your birthday?" Ashley asked.

Skip finished signing for the balloons. He grinned at us. "No, but I just got my pilot's license. So today is a big day for me. This year at the air show I won't just be watching."

"That's awesome," I told him.

"We should get started," Ashley said. She pulled out a sketch pad. "I want to draw the layout of the room on paper, Mary-Kate. Why don't you hunt for clues?"

I started to make my way slowly around the room. I was looking for anything that seemed out of place. Even a little scrap of paper could be the clue that brings a case together.

I should have done this yesterday, I realized. The room had been cleaned last night. That meant most of the clues had probably been swept away.

"What exactly are you looking for?" Jamie asked.

I gave a little jump. I didn't know he'd come up behind me. "I'm not sure yet," I said. "Why don't you go talk to Skip some more?"

If I found something, I didn't want anyone to know except Ashley. That's because anyone else might be a suspect in the case.

"Oh. Okay." Jamie sounded a little hurt. He picked at a scab on his skinny elbow as he wandered off.

I finished circling the room. Then I started again. This time I really studied every inch of the floor. I was extra careful in the corners.

I spotted something in the third corner. It was a little piece of red wire. "Yes!" I

whispered. I didn't know if it had anything to do with our case. But I *did* know that it didn't belong. I pulled a plastic sandwich bag out of my backpack. Then I carefully placed the wire inside.

The last corner of the room was empty. I decided to see how Ashley was doing.

I stepped up behind my sister and studied her drawing. "Wow, you even put in the drinking fountain."

"Hey, you never know what's going to be important," Ashley reminded me.

"You keep drawing while I start a list of suspects," I said. "You can talk while you draw, right?"

"And chew gum, too," Ashley joked.

I glanced back at Skip and Jamie. They were looking at an old black-and-white picture on the wall. Good. It meant they weren't watching us.

"I say suspect number one is Mr. Frost," I told Ashley. I wrote his name down in my

notebook. A lot of times I use a mini tape recorder for notes. But I like to *look* at suspects' names. It helps me think.

"Definitely," Ashley said, nodding. "Mr. Frost wants to buy the plane. If people are afraid of the *Phantom*, they'll stop coming to the museum. Then Terri will probably sell the plane."

"Who else?" I had an idea, but I didn't want to say it.

"Um, maybe we should put down Jamie," Ashley answered. "He's been totally nice and everything, but—"

"But if the museum sells the plane, he gets the money," I finished for her. "And he seems to like money a *lot*."

"The only thing is, Jamie didn't know that he'd get the money until yesterday," Ashley said. "And Terri told us the first weird haunting happened two weeks ago."

"Maybe Jamie only *acted* surprised," I said.

Ashley nodded and I added Jamie's name to the list. There were still two more names I wanted to write. But I didn't think Ashley wanted to hear them.

"Those two are the only suspects I can think of. Until we get some more clues, anyway. How about you?" Ashley asked.

I tapped my pen against my notebook. Should I tell Ashley what I was thinking? Or not? I tapped faster and faster—until the pen flew out of my fingers.

I bent down to get it. When I got up, Ashley was staring at me. "Come on, Mary-Kate. Whatever it is, say it."

Sometimes it's as if Ashley can almost read my mind. "There should be two more names on the list," I said. "The Duncan brothers!"

Ashley groaned. "There are no such things as ghosts. We've talked about this a zillion times."

"But we're detectives," I argued. "And

that means we have to keep open minds. I'm not saying that ghosts are real. But we have to at least *think* about it."

"You want a pair of ghosts on the suspect list? Fine," Ashley said. "But I'll stick to living people. Fair?"

"Fair," I answered, shrugging.

"Okay. I'm done," Ashley said. "Let's go hang out with Skip and Jamie. We can just wait for whatever's going to happen."

Skip and Jamie both smiled at us as we headed over. But Jamie's smile suddenly left his face. "Hey!" he cried. "Something's happening!"

I whirled around and looked up at the *Phantom*. Red letters were appearing on the side of the plane. H-E-L-P-U-S.

"Help us!" Ashley exclaimed.

A terrible moan came from the plane. It was almost as if someone was answering her.

Skip bravely stepped forward. "Who

are you?" he called out.

"Elllioooot Duuuncan," a voice groaned.

"Heeennnnrrry Duuuncan," another voice wailed.

I gasped. The ghosts really were the Duncan brothers!

Just then, more words started forming on the side of the *Phantom:* HELP US, MARY-KATE AND ASHLEY.

I grabbed Ashley's hand. She grabbed mine at the same time.

"How can we help? What do you want us to do?" I called.

The first words disappeared. Almost instantly another message took its place.

FLY THE PLANE. OR SUFFER THE PAIN.

5

LEFT HANGING

"**S**uffer the pain," I read out loud. I stared at the words on the side of the *Phantom*. I didn't take my eyes off them until they were gone.

My heart thumped as I let out my breath. I didn't even realize I had been holding it.

"What does that mean?" I cried. "Tell us how to help."

But there was no wailed reply. No new message appeared on the plane.

"We should think about the words," Skip

said. I could see his fingers shaking. "The ghosts want their plane to be flown."

Ashley frowned, the way she does when she's thinking hard. "So you think if someone flies the *Phantom*—"

Skip didn't let her finish. "Yes!" he cried. "That's what the ghosts want. For their plane to be in the sky again. That's where it belongs. And the air show would be the perfect place! It's next week!"

I could tell that the thought of the *Flying Phantom* actually flying made Skip happy. So happy he wasn't scared anymore.

I still had the creeps. I inched closer to Ashley. "Don't you think it's spooky that the ghosts know our names?" I whispered.

"*Somebody* knows our names. That's for sure," she whispered back. "But I'm still betting our suspect is no ghost." She turned to Skip. "Mary-Kate and I need to look at the plane up close. Is there a way for us to get up there?"

"We use the catwalk for cleaning and repairs." Skip pointed to a narrow walkway running along the wall next to the *Phantom*. "But I don't know if it's such a good idea."

"Of course it's not a good idea!" Jamie cried. "It's a very bad idea. It's the worst idea anyone ever had."

"We're detectives. We have to find clues," I told him.

And I really hoped we would get some. Nice, solid, couldn't-possibly-be-from-a-ghost clues.

"I'll bring the ladder around," Skip said. He headed out of the room.

"You do know that the ghosts are in that plane, don't you?" Jamie said to us. "You inside. Ghosts inside. Doesn't that make you think this might not be a good move?"

Ashley opened her mouth to reply. But Jamie rushed on. "Don't think I'm going up there to protect you, either. I came in here today to look out for you. But I'm not—"

"Jamie, you don't have to," I cut him off. "We've done lots more dangerous things than this with no problem." I was glad he didn't ask me to tell him about one. Because right that second, I couldn't think of any.

I heard the sound of wheels on the wood floor. A moment later, Skip appeared. He was rolling a tall ladder in front of him. He moved it under the catwalk. Then he locked the ladder in place with metal hooks that went into two rings in the wall.

"You two go up first. I'll be right behind you," Skip said.

Ashley started up the ladder. I went next.

"You can still just turn around," Jamie called from the floor.

We kept climbing. As soon as we reached the catwalk, I stretched out my hand and touched the side of the *Phantom*. My fingers were over the spot where a

piece of the message had been.

But the plane's side was dry and cool.

I didn't feel anything at all that was wet or sticky, like paint—or blood.

"Don't climb on board yet. I want you to put on these safety harnesses first," Skip instructed. He handed one to me and one to Ashley. "Then I'll hook you to the catwalk."

I helped Ashley tighten the harness's straps around her. Then she helped me. Skip attached lines from the harnesses to the catwalk. "But no bungee jumping," he ordered.

"Right!" I turned to Ashley. "I want to sit in the pilot's seat!"

I carefully climbed into the plane. Then I settled into the open pilot's seat. Ashley sat down next to me.

I ran my fingers over one of the dials in the control panel. For a moment I wasn't thinking about ghosts or mysteries. I was

thinking about how awesome it was to be sitting in the *Phantom*.

"Do you see anything?" Skip called.

"Not yet," Ashley and I answered at the same time.

I divided the little cockpit into four parts. It's a trick that our great-grandma Olive taught us. She's a detective, too. And she says it's easier to look for clues one section at a time.

I started my clue search with the control panel. Everything looked all right. At least as far as I could tell.

But then, the needle on one of the controls started to jump back and forth.

"Oh, no," I gasped. "That is definitely *not* good."

The floor of the cockpit began to shake.

"Mary-Kate, do you feel that?" Ashley cried. Her voice was shaky, too.

"Yes!" I called back. I couldn't get out another word. The whole plane was shak-

ing so hard my teeth slammed together. I grabbed the edge of my seat with both hands. My heart thumped double-time.

"Fly the plane! Or suffer the pain!" two voices wailed.

The Phantom gave an extra-hard jerk. My eyes went to the metal cables that attached the plane to the ceiling.

They began to creak!

"Oh, no!" I shouted. "They're going to snap!"

6

MISSING EVIDENCE

"**H**elp!" I screamed.

"Hold on, Mary-Kate," Ashley yelled. "It's stopping."

I realized my teeth weren't slamming together anymore. And the cockpit floor wasn't trembling. We were still moving. But we were swinging now, not shaking.

"You're okay now," Skip yelled.

Whoosh! Whoosh! Whoosh!

Each swing was a little shorter.

Finally the *Phantom* stopped swinging

and hung still on its cables.

Skip stood on the catwalk. His eyes were wide with alarm. He rushed to the plane and helped me out of the cockpit. Then he pulled Ashley out of the gunner's seat. "You must be pretty shaken up," he said.

Ashley took a deep breath. "We're okay, aren't we, Mary-Kate?" she asked.

"Yeah," I answered. I struggled out of my harness. Then I started down the ladder. I wanted to get some space between the *Phantom* and me. Fast!

"It feels good to have the ground under my sneakers," Ashley said.

"I could kiss the floor!" I agreed.

Ashley turned to Jamie. "Did you see anything strange?" she asked him.

He snorted. "What? Like a haunted airplane?"

"No, no," Ashley said. "I mean like anyone else coming into the room."

Terri rushed into the room. "The guard saw the whole thing on the security video cameras. He told me what happened," she said. "Are you all right?"

"We're fine," Ashley answered.

"Don't believe it," Jamie muttered. He shoved his hair off his forehead. "They're both crazy."

"I didn't think you girls would be in danger," Terri said. She tugged on the end of her French braid. "I don't want you working on this case anymore."

"No way!" I told her. I didn't have to check with Ashley. We never quit a case.

"We'd really like to go on," Ashley said. "Please! We'll stay out of the plane. We promise."

"Well, all right," Terri gave in. She sighed. "I really do need your help. Ticket sales are way down today. I think the *Phantom* is the cause. Look at this."

Terri held out a copy of the *Washington*

Reporter. Ashley took the paper and read the headline out loud. "*Flying Phantom* Possible Threat to Museum Visitors."

I started to read over her shoulder. "They interviewed Walter Frost," I said. "He says that it isn't safe for anyone to be in the same building with the *Phantom*."

"They talked with Angelina, too," Ashley added. "She says that this is the work of ghosts and that she could solve the whole problem by contacting them. But the museum won't let her."

"I think we're done in here," I told Terri. "Can we look at some more of the videotapes?"

"Come with me," Terri said. She turned and headed for the exit. "Don't let anyone near the *Phantom* today, Skip," she called over her shoulder. "And tell everyone not to talk to any reporters. I don't want another story in the paper."

I gave Jamie a little wave good-bye.

"We'll see you later!"

Terri led the way to her office. "Are there any special tapes you want to see?" she asked.

"I want to check out the tape of the hours *before* something strange happened to the *Phantom*," Ashley answered. "Maybe Mary-Kate and I will see someone doing some kind of setup."

"I'll have to get those tapes from our museum guard," Terri answered. She opened the door to her office. "Make yourselves at home."

I moved a box of slides off one of the chairs and sat down. "Do you still think someone alive is behind this mystery?" I asked Ashley. "Even after what just happened?"

She nodded. "We have lots of good suspects," she reminded me. "Suspects who aren't ghosts. I even have a new one."

"Who?" I asked.

"Angelina Ritter," Ashley answered. "That article put her name in the paper. It was like an ad for Angelina. I bet she'll get a lot of new customers now."

"Hmmm. Great-grandma Olive always says to look for the motive," I said. "Angelina's reason for doing something bad might be money."

"People commit crimes for money all the time," Ashley agreed. "Maybe she's doing this to get more customers."

"That makes sense," I said.

Ashley frowned. "Every time we talk about money, I think of Jamie."

I nodded. "Have you noticed his T-shirts?" I asked. "Yesterday, a hundred-dollar bill. Today, a piggy bank. It's as if money is all he thinks about."

"Yeah." Ashley shook her head. "At least he's not our only suspect. We have Angelina now. And we still have Mr. Frost. Maybe we should even put Skip on our list."

"Why Skip?" I asked. I couldn't think of any motive for him.

"Skip would love to see the plane in the air," Ashley said. "And that was part of the message. Fly the plane."

"We're starting to get too many suspects. And not enough clues," I said. "All we have is this." I held up the plastic sandwich bag. Ashley studied the piece of red wire inside. "I'm not even sure it's a clue," I added.

"I think I hear Terri coming back," Ashley said. "Maybe the tapes will tell us something new."

I crossed my fingers. So did Ashley.

"There's Skip with his walkie-talkie again," I said.

Ashley made a little mark on our score sheet. So far Skip had been in every tape we'd looked at. But that was normal. He worked at the museum.

"Mr. Frost is on this tape, too," Ashley

commented. "Did you notice that he always wears the same suit?"

I kept my eyes on the little television. "Oooh. Angelina should be glad Terri isn't watching this with us," I said. On the screen, Angelina had headed over to some tourists. She was writing her phone number down for them.

Ashley made a mark under Angelina's name. Angelina already had several marks. So did Jamie.

"Hey! Here's something weird," Ashley said.

I leaned forward and peered at the screen. "What?"

"Remember the drawing I made of the exhibit room?" Ashley asked. "There were *three* video cameras."

"Right," I answered. "But what does that matter?"

"It looks like all the tapes have been filmed from *two* cameras. The one right

over the entrance, and the one on the wall across from the catwalk."

I thought about it. "You're right!" I exclaimed. "None of the tapes are from the camera on the same side as the catwalk!"

"Terri said these were all of the tapes," Ashley answered. "You know what this means?"

"Actually, no. I don't," I admitted.

"It means someone has stolen an important piece of evidence!" Ashley told me.

7

SEARCHING THE SUSPECTS

"**I** think our first stop should be Mr. Frost's house," Ashley said. We headed out of Terri's office. "He's our number-one suspect."

"We should talk to Angelina, too," I said. "I want to hear what she thinks about the ghosts. I wonder if she thinks all they want is to see their plane in the air."

Ashley groaned. "Mary-Kate."

"I mean, *if* this case turns out to have any ghosts in it at all," I said quickly. "I'm

keeping an open mind."

Ashley stared across the museum lobby. I followed her gaze. She was looking at Jamie's T-shirt stand. He'd opened it up while we were watching the tapes.

"I guess we have to ask Jamie a few questions, too. We should keep an open mind about *all* our suspects," she said.

"Yeah. Even though Jamie's been so nice, we have to do it." I led the way over. "So have you been making big bucks today?" I asked him.

He shook his head. "No. I've lost money. Someone returned a T-shirt. I don't blame him. Who wants a shirt of a haunted plane?" he said. "And I think people heard that I'm related to the ghosts. They're afraid of me."

"Don't worry, Jamie. If the museum sells the *Phantom*, you'll be rich," Ashley told him.

Jamie's eyes lit up. "Wouldn't that be

awesome? I can't believe I even have a shot at the kind of money." He grinned. "Millionaire. The word even *tastes* good."

"So, um, no one ever explained that the museum didn't really own the *Phantom*?" I asked.

I watched Jamie carefully. I wanted to see if he blushed. Or looked at his feet. Or started scratching. Or did anything else that made him look guilty—like picking at that scab on his elbow.

But Jamie looked me straight in the eye. "The only person who could have told me is probably my dad," Jamie answered. "But he died when I was little. And Mom doesn't know anything about the plane."

"We'll solve this case," Ashley promised him. "Then you'll be selling a ton of T-shirts again. And no one will be afraid to get close to a relative of the famous Duncan brothers. They'll just think it's cool!"

I hoped she was right.

"What are we going to say to Mr. Frost?" I asked. "What reason should we give for being here?" I stared up at his huge pink mansion.

"I'll ask if he remembers anything more about what happened yesterday," Ashley said. "And you can—"

"Search for the missing videotapes," I finished for her.

Ashley rang the doorbell. It sounded like an elephant trumpeting. A few moments later Mr. Frost opened the door. "Hello, Mr. Frost," Ashley said. "We were wondering if we could ask you a few questions about—"

"About the haunted plane?" he interrupted. "About the plane that is putting lives in danger? All because Terri Napoli doesn't want to sell it to me?"

"Excuse me—may I use the bathroom?" I asked.

"Sure. It's up the stairs on the right,"

Mr. Frost answered, pointing.

I hurried off. I could hear Mr. Frost still talking to Ashley behind me as I started up the wide staircase.

At the top of the stairs, I opened the first door I came to. A blast of cold air hit me in the face. I had to cover my mouth with both hands to hold back a scream of surprise.

An enormous, quivering mass of *meat* stood in the center of the floor. It was so tall it almost touched the ceiling. I noticed a small gold sign on the wall and walked up to it. The smell of the meat was so strong it made me gag.

"First sculpture made entirely of Spam," I read out loud. "Oh, ick." I backed out of the room and shut the door.

I continued down the hall to the left. When I got to the next door, I opened it slowly. Three long, long tables filled the room. On each table were rows of huge glass jars.

I hurried over to the closest one and peered inside. My stomach turned over. Inside the jar was a snake with two heads. I read the gold sign. FIRST TWO-HEADED RATTLE-SNAKE.

I'd seen enough. I left without checking out the other jars.

I rushed down the hall and into the next room. "Yes!" I cried. The perfect place to hunt for the missing videotapes.

First I checked out the big TV in the corner. There were no tapes in the VCR. The security video wasn't in the tape cabinet, either.

Next, I headed for the desk. Right on top was a drawing. It was of Mr. Frost's mansion.

In the drawing a smaller building had been added behind the big one. They were connected by a glassed-in bridge. Mr. Frost was planning to add more rooms to his house.

A second drawing lay under the first.

This one showed the smaller building from the inside. Most of the second building was one huge room. A neat label said what the room would hold. The *Flying Phantom*!

I tapped my chin thoughtfully with my finger. The drawing told me two things.

One—Mr. Frost wanted the *Phantom* very badly.

Two—he was very sure he was going to get it.

8

ANGRY GHOSTS

I pulled Ashley up the walkway to Angelina's little house. "I really want to talk to Angelina about ghost stuff."

"And I want to try and find out if she's gotten a lot of new customers lately," Ashley said.

It was later that day. I hadn't found the missing videotapes at Mr. Frost's house. But that didn't mean they weren't there.

I rang the doorbell and waited.

"Uh-oh, Mary-Kate. Look at this," Ashley

said. She pointed to a sheet of paper taped next to the door.

I leaned closer to read the small print. "It says Angelina owes three months rent. If she doesn't pay it in three days, she has to move out! Poor Angelina."

Ashley shook her head. "She needs money. That means she has a really good motive for making the *Phantom* look haunted." Ashlely shrugged. "If more people believe in ghosts, Angelina gets more customers."

I rang the doorbell again. There was still no answer.

We turned around to leave and saw Angelina rushing up the walkway. Her dozens of crystal necklaces kept knocking into each other.

"You are here for help with the ghosts! How wonderful!" she exclaimed. She came up the steps and opened her door. "You have come to the right place," she said.

"Angelina knows ghosts."

Inside, I filled her in on the latest message from the ghosts. I described how hard the plane shook when Ashley and I were inside.

"I knew this would happen," she said. "The Duncan brothers are angry."

"I'm glad you have time to talk to us," Ashley told her. "We thought you might be too busy."

"I do have a lot of customers right now," Angelina said. "I've been getting many calls since this morning's newspaper story." She led us down to a doorway with a curtain of crystals hanging over it. They clicked and clacked as we stepped through.

It was hard to see anything. Angelina hadn't turned on any lights. And the windows were draped with velvet curtains.

"I work by candlelight," she explained. She began lighting candles as she spoke. "It is more welcoming to the spirits."

"Why?" Ashley asked.

"It makes it easier for them to see us. And for us to see them," Angelina explained. "Come sit down at the table."

Ashley and I sat across from her. I wondered if any ghosts were watching us right then.

Angelina rested her hands on a large crystal ball and gazed at us. "As I said, it is clear that the ghosts of the Duncan brothers are angry. And angry ghosts are very dangerous."

"How do we make them happy again? We want them to be happy!" I burst out. Ashley didn't say anything.

"I need to contact them in the museum. The ghosts will tell me exactly what they want. We must take action soon or else—"

The doorbell rang.

"Oh, goody!" Angelina cried. "Another customer. They must have read the newspaper!" She leaped up. "You two stay right

here." She hurried away.

I stood up. "Maybe Angelina has the missing videotapes. We should look around."

Ashley began poking through a stack of tapes on top of a small TV. "I can't read these titles. It's too dark," she said. She turned on a light and checked the videos. "No. It's not here."

I picked up a book sitting on a wooden bookstand. "Oh, wow, look at this!" I cried. The book was called *The Secrets of Ghosts*.

"I'm too busy looking at *this*," Ashley answered. She stood staring at some wicked-looking masks hanging on the wall.

I opened the book. It didn't take long to find the chapter I was interested in. "When Ghosts Become Angry."

My throat got dry as I began to read. I swallowed hard. "Ashley, listen to this. When ghosts get mad they can make blisters appear on people's skin. They can make someone's hair fall out. They can—"

"Mary-Kate, I've said it before and I'll say it again," Ashley said. "I. Do. Not. Believe. In. Ghosts." She flopped down into a big chair against the wall.

That's when it appeared!

"Ashley! Ashley! Ashley!" That's all I could get out.

"What?" she asked.

My hand shook as I pointed at the ghost.

She turned and saw it, too.

A white figure stood in the middle of the room. It had dark eyes and floating white hair.

It was staring right at Ashley!

Its mouth opened. A piercing wail filled the room. Then it raised its hands. It had claws where its fingers should be.

"Run, Ashley!" I cried. "Now! Now! Run, run, run!"

And she did run. Straight for the ghost!

9

THE SHAKY CONCLUSION

"**R**un *away*!" I yelled.

Then, I blinked. The ghost was gone!

"Where did it go?" Ashley cried. She stared at the wall where the ghost had been.

"It's on your back," I answered slowly.

"That's not funny!" Ashley exclaimed. "Where is it?"

"That's really where it is!" I told her. I suddenly understood. "It's not a real ghost. It's a movie ghost. I can see a piece of it on the back of your shirt. You must be standing in front of a movie projector."

I grabbed Ashley by the elbow and pulled her a few feet to the right. The ghost came back onto the wall again.

"It *is* just a movie." Ashley reached out and touched the ghost on the wall.

I turned around and studied the opposite wall. "I think I see the projector," I said. It was almost hidden by the vines coming off a pot of ivy hanging above it.

I climbed onto the big chair Ashley had been sitting in. Then I shoved away the ivy so Ashley could see the whole camera setup.

"Good work, Mary-Kate," she said.

"Thanks." I stepped from the arm of the chair to the seat.

The ghost on the wall changed. This time it was a light-blue man. He raised his hand to his face and wiped away a tear.

"There must be some kind of remote control in this chair," Ashley said. "The first

ghost appeared when I sat down. And it switched to the next ghost when you stepped on the cushion."

I hopped off the chair and pulled up the cushion. "You're right, Ashley," I exclaimed. I held up a little box about the size of a walkie-talkie. It had lots of buttons.

I pushed one of the buttons. A low whispering filled the room. I hit another button. The crystal ball on the table began to glow.

"I can't believe this!" I said. "Angelina is a big faker. She tricks people into thinking ghosts are real."

"So she can get their money," Ashley agreed. She reached out her hand. "Let me try the remote."

I handed it to her. She punched a button—and the table started to shake. "Just like the *Phantom*," she whispered.

"How is it doing that?" I asked.

"Let's find out." Ashley and I crawled under the table.

"Check this out." Ashley grabbed my hand and pressed it against a metal box attached underneath the table. It was shaking so hard that it was making the table shake, too.

I scooted closer so I could study the box. A piece of red wire stuck out from one end. "Hey, that's just like the wire I found in the museum!" I exclaimed.

When I touched the box again, the table stopped shaking.

"I bet there are some boxes like this in the *Phantom*," Ashley said.

"And I bet that the third video camera isn't a camera. It's a projector!" I said.

"Of course!" Ashley cried. "It's right across from the plane. It could have projected the words we saw onto the *Phantom*'s side."

"That explains why we couldn't find the tapes from that camera," I said. "There *is* no camera there!"

Ashley gave an excited little bounce. "This is great. Now we know exactly how the *Phantom* is being haunted."

"And we know who is haunting it, too. Angelina," I said.

"Shhh!" Ashley said. "She'll be back any second."

"I wonder how she hid the projector in the museum," I said in a quieter voice. "It would be hard to set up without anyone seeing her."

Ashley snapped her fingers. "Maybe Angelina is partners with one of our other suspects."

"Let's go over them again," I said.

Ashley took out her notebook and flipped it open. "Well, there's Jamie."

"Because he loves money," I added. "And he knows the museum really well. He could have helped Angelina hide her projector. The question is, when did he find out he'd get the money if the *Phantom* got sold?"

"Right," Ashley agreed. "If he really found out when *we* found out—"

"Then he isn't the one making the plane seem haunted," I finished for her. "He has no motive. In fact, the haunting is hurting his T-shirt business."

"But if he found out *before*—" Ashley said.

"Then he'd have a very, very good motive," I finished again. "Tons, and tons, and tons of money."

"Okay, suspect number two: Skip." Ashley drummed her fingers on the metal box. I could tell she was thinking hard. "He wants the plane to fly. And that's what the ghosts asked for."

"Except now we know there are no ghosts. So maybe *Skip* was the one sending those messages," I said. "It would be totally easy for him to set up a projector."

"He *did* just get his pilot's license," Ashley added. "And he's really excited about the air show."

"He even said it would be the perfect place to fly the *Phantom*," I said. I put my hand to my forehead. "Ow. My brain is starting to hurt from too much thinking."

"Suspect number three: Mr. Frost," Ashley said. "He's already planning a new room for the *Phantom*."

I heard footsteps in the hall. "Angelina's coming back," I whispered.

Ashley and I scrambled out from under the table. She hurried across the room and stuck the remote under the chair cushion.

"Fluff the ivy," I said. Ashley arranged the vines so only the lens of the camera was showing again. Then she raced back over to me. We both sat down at the table.

As the doorknob turned, I had a great idea. I leaned close to Ashley. "I just thought of a way to find out exactly which of our suspects is behind the hauntings. Let me do the talking. And agree with me—no matter what I say."

Ashley nodded as Angelina hurried in.

"Sorry to keep you waiting so long," she said.

"Was it a customer?" Ashley asked.

Angelina played with one of her crystal necklaces. "No," she admitted. "It was someone from the gas company."

"Ashley and I had a chance to talk," I jumped in. "And we decided you're right. We need to contact the ghosts. Can you do it tomorrow night?"

10

TRICKS AND LIES

"**D**o we really have to do this?" Terri asked. She tucked a stray section of hair back into her braid.

"Definitely," Ashley answered. "It will tell us everything we need to know."

Walter Frost walked into the exhibit room wearing the same suit as always. "Hi, Mr. Frost," I called. "Thanks for coming."

"This will be my first meeting with ghosts," he answered. "I can't resist a first." He turned to Terri. "I hope you'll come to

your senses tonight and agree to sell me the *Phantom*."

He spotted Jamie coming into the room. "I brought my checkbook tonight, young man. If we can get Terri to agree, you could walk out of here a multi-millionaire."

"*Multi*-millionaire," Jamie repeated. He swallowed hard. "Wow!"

"Everybody's here except for Angelina," Ashley said.

Terri put her hand to her ear. "She's coming. I hear her crystals clacking together in the hall."

"I hope the plan works," I whispered in Ashley's ear.

Then Angelina walked in. "Let us prepare," she said in a low, serious voice.

A few moments later, we were surrounded by darkness. The *Phantom* glowed in spotlights above.

"Now we must form the circle," Angelina said.

She sat on the floor in the center of the room. Terri sat on one side of her. Mr. Frost sat on the other. I sat next to Terri. Ashley sat next to me. Then came Skip and Jamie.

Angelina placed a thick red candle in the center of our circle. Then she lit it.

"I will need complete silence once we begin," Angelina told us. "And it is important that no one leaves the circle. Very, very important."

"What will happen if we do?" Jamie asked.

"You could get sucked into the spirit world," Angelina answered. "And it might not be possible to get you back."

Jamie scooted closer to the candle. I could tell he was nervous. I was nervous, too. *It's all a trick*, I reminded myself. *Angelina is a total faker.*

Angelina gazed around the circle. "Let's begin."

She began to swing a metal ball back

and forth again. "Elliott Duncan. Henry Duncan," she said. "We know you have something to tell us. Join us," she said. Her voice was low and strong. "We came here tonight to listen. Please join us."

The *Phantom* began to shake.

"Welcome!" Angelina cried. "You honor us with your visit."

Two voices began to wail.

A drop of sweat ran from the base of my neck all the way down my back.

"Elliott and Henry, we are listening. Speak to us!" Angelina urged.

"Someone lies. Now someone dies!" Jamie shouted.

"What?" Terri demanded.

Jamie pointed at the *Phantom*. The words had appeared in blood-red letters.

SOMEONE LIES. NOW SOMEONE DIES.

"No. Oh, no," Angelina moaned.

Her hand flew up to her heart—then she fell to the floor.

11

CASE CLOSED!

An instant later the spotlights directed on the plane went out. Someone knocked over the candle. It went out, too. And Mr. Frost let out a scream in the dark.

"Angelina's dead!" he cried.

"She's not dead. She fainted," Terri snapped. "I have a little bottle of water in my purse. Would you get it, Mary-Kate? I'll turn on the lights."

I heard her move away through the big room. "Ouch. Ow!" she grumbled as she

crashed into something hard.

I began getting used to seeing in the dark. I found the purse and splashed a little water on Angelina's face. "Wake up," I said.

"...Wasn't supposed to happen," Angelina muttered as her eyes opened. "It wasn't supposed to say that."

I caught Ashley's eye. Things were working out well. So far.

Angelina sat up. She held her head. "Oh!" she groaned.

Slowly, she stood and glared at Skip. "What are you trying to do?" she demanded angrily. "Scare me to death?"

We all stared at Skip. He stood up quickly. "Me? Why would I want to do that?"

"To keep me quiet!" she shot back. "So I won't tell everyone what you've done!"

"You're crazy!" he yelled at her. "It was you! I'm not the one who switched the—"

He cut himself off. But it was too late. His face turned a bright red.

"Switched the what?" Terri asked.

"The slide!" Angelina shrieked. "He's trying to scare me. He wants me to stay away now that the world thinks the plane is haunted."

"He didn't switch the slide!" Ashley said.

"We did it," I put in.

Angelina and Skip turned sharply toward us. Their eyes were wide with surprise.

"What's going on?" Terri asked.

"Ashley and I figured out that someone was making the *Phantom* appear haunted," I began.

"We knew whoever it was used a projector to put messages on the side of the *Phantom*. So Mary-Kate and I made a message of our own," Ashley went on. "We put it on a slide."

"This afternoon, we switched the slides," I said. "Then all we had to do was wait. And watch."

"Wait for what?" Jamie asked

"Well, Angelina wasn't expecting the message she saw," Ashley answered. "You all heard her. She said, 'It wasn't supposed to say that.'"

"Which means that she knew exactly what message was going to appear on the plane," I explained. "There's only one way she could have known that."

"If she was one of the people who was making the plane look haunted," Ashley explained.

"*One* of the people?" Terri repeated. She stared over at Skip.

"We knew Angelina couldn't have pulled this off alone. We figured that the person helping her would be just as upset by the message switch," Ashley told her.

"We hoped he'd do something to give himself away," I said, looking at Skip. "And he definitely did."

"Is this true, Skip?" Terri asked. "Are the girls right?"

Skip nodded sadly.

"I don't understand. Why?" Terri glanced from Angelina to Skip.

"Angelina, you wanted more customers, right?" I asked her.

She nodded.

"Skip's motive wasn't as clear," Ashley said. "But we think he wanted to fly the *Phantom* in the air show."

Skip ran his hands over his hair. "You're right. I've been amazed by the *Phantom* my whole life. That's why I became a museum guide here."

He glanced over his shoulder at the *Phantom*. Then he turned back to us. "At first it was enough just to be in the same room with it. Then I started thinking about flying the plane myself."

"So you got your pilot's license," I said.

"And you and Angelina came up with the plan that would get both of you what you wanted," Ashley added.

"Oh, Skip," Terri said. "Don't you care about the museum at all?"

"Not as much as I care about the *Phantom*," Skip admitted. "I only wanted to fly it once. Then I would have found a way to prove to people it wasn't haunted. I don't want people to be afraid of it."

"Skip, I'm going to have to let you go," Terri told him.

"You're firing me?" Skip asked. "I'll never be able to see the *Phantom* again?" He looked as if he was about to cry.

"You can visit it," Terri answered. "But first I want you to talk to a reporter and tell them exactly what you did." She turned to Angelina. "You, too."

"But if I do, I won't ever get any more customers," Angelina wailed. "No one will trust me."

"I'll hire you," Mr. Frost volunteered. "I like sneaky people. I could use you to help me get some more of my firsts."

He grinned at Ashley and me. "I could create a space for you in my collection, too," he offered. "I bet you two are the first twin detectives ever."

"No way, Mr. Frost," Jamie told him. "The twins can't be locked away in your mansion. The world needs Mary-Kate and Ashley!"

"Yes!" Ashley and I gave each other a high five. We'd cracked another case!

Hi from both of us,

Great-grandma Olive gave us a scary treat this Halloween—a night full of adventure at a haunted fun house called Creepy Castle!

But our adventure turned into a mystery when our friends started disappearing, one by one. Soon Ashley and I were the only two left. And if we didn't crack this case soon, the next visitors to vanish would be us!

Think this mystery sounds like a scream? Take a look at the next page for a sneak peek at *The New Adventures of Mary-Kate & Ashley: The Case of the Creepy Castle.*

See you next time!

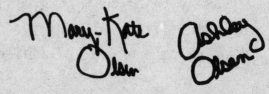

A sneak peek at our next mystery…

The Case Of The
Creepy Castle

I stared at the witch. Was she a good witch, or a bad witch?

"We're looking for our friend Tim," Ashley said. "Have you seen him?"

"No," the witch said. "But if you look closely, a clue might appear in my brew."

Ashley and I peered into the cauldron.

I shrugged. "Looks like alphabet soup."

"That's the whole idea!" the witch cackled. "The letters will spell out the answer to your question!" She held out the big wooden handle. "Anyone want to help me stir?"

No one answered.

The witch smiled and pointed to Samantha. "You can help me," she said. "A cat is always a witch's best friend."

Samantha looked down at her cat costume. "M-me?" she squeaked.

The witch hooked her finger. "Here, kitty, kitty!"

Samantha gulped. She grabbed the wooden spoon and moved it in big circles.

"Bubble, bubble, boil to the brim!" the witch began to chant. "Help us find our good friend—Tim!"

"This is nuts," I whispered to Ashley. "There's no such thing as a magic br—"

I never finished my sentence. A thick souplike fog filled the room. So thick that I couldn't see a thing!

"Mary-Kate!" Ashley called.

"I'm here!" I shouted back.

"So am I!" Patty yelled.

I expected Samantha to answer next—but she didn't!

"Samantha, are you there?" I demanded.

No answer. The fog began to thin out. I could see Ashley and Patty through the mist. But as I looked around the parlor I saw that the witch was gone.

And so was Samantha!

BRING IT ON!

MARY-KATE OLSEN ASHLEY OLSEN

SWITCHING GOALS

DUALSTAR VIDEO

Outta-site!
marykateandashley.com
Register Now

OWN IT ONLY ON VIDEO!

DUALSTAR
VIDEO

Double the fashion!
Double the fun!

with Mary-Kate & Ashley Fashion Dolls

Mary-Kate and ASHLEY

Ride with Mary-Kate

ance with Ashley

Join their slumber party

GaMe GiRLS

Mary-Kate & Ashley's
Magical Mystery Mall

October 2000

Available Now

Outta-site!
marykateandashley.com
Register Now

TM & © 2000 Dualstar Entertainment Group Inc.

Check out
the Reading Room on
marykateandashley.com
for an exclusive
online chapter preview
of our upcoming book!

DUALSTAR
ONLINE

This Book Belongs to...

Kali Parr